W9-AMS-053

Dear Parents and Teachers,

In an easy-reader format, **My Readers** introduce classic stories to children who are learning to read. Although favorite characters and time-tested tales are the basis for **My Readers**, the books tell completely new stories and are freshly and beautifully illustrated.

My Readers are available in three levels:

1 **Level One** is for the emergent reader and features repetitive language and word clues in the illustrations.

2 **Level Two** is for more advanced readers who still need support saying and understanding some words. Stories are longer with word clues in the illustrations.

3 **Level Three** is for independent, fluent readers who enjoy working out occasional unfamiliar words. The stories are longer and divided into chapters.

Encourage children to select books based on interests, not reading levels. Read aloud with children, showing them how to use the illustrations for clues. With adult guidance and rereading, children will eventually read the desired book on their own.

Here are some ways you might want to use this book with children:

- Talk about the title and the cover illustrations. Encourage the child to use these to predict what the story is about.
- Discuss the interior illustrations and try to piece together a story based on the pictures. Does the child want to change or adjust his first prediction?
- After children reread a story, suggest they retell or act out a favorite part.

My Readers will not only help children become readers, they will serve as an introduction to some of the finest classic children's books available today.

—LAURA ROBB
Educator and Reading Consultant

For Debbie
—B. F.

An Imprint of Macmillan Children's Publishing Group

Distributed in Canada by H.B. Fenn and Company Ltd.
Printed in January 2011 in China by Toppan Leefung Printing Ltd., Dongguan City, Guangdong Province.
For information, address Square Fish, 175 Fifth Avenue, New York, NY 10010.

Library of Congress Cataloging-in-Publication Data Available

ISBN: 978-0-312-64722-3 (hardcover)
1 3 5 7 9 10 8 6 4 2

ISBN: 978-0-312-64723-0 (paperback)
1 3 5 7 9 10 8 6 4 2

Book design by Patrick Collins/Véronique Lefèvre Sweet

Square Fish logo designed by Filomena Tuosto

First Edition: 2011

1 3 5 7 9 10 8 6 4 2

www.squarefishbooks.com
www.mackids.com

This is a Level 3 book

LEXILE 520L

Black Beauty

Stolen!

story by **SUSAN HILL**

illustrated by **BILL FARNSWORTH**

inspired by **ANNA SEWELL's** ***Black Beauty***

SQUARE FISH

Macmillan Children's Publishing Group

New York

Chapter One
A Song

My name is Black Beauty.

But when my new owner bought me,

he gave me a new name.

I pull a cab for Jerry,

and he calls me Jack.

Pulling a cab
on the crowded streets of London
is hard work.
I am lucky that Jerry is a kind master.

At the end of the day,
Jerry always gives me a treat—
a bit of apple or sweet, crunchy carrot.
Best of all, Jerry sings to me.

One night, Jerry sang a song
I liked very much.
The words made me feel calm
and peaceful.
Softly, Jerry sang.
"Do your best and leave the rest,
'twill all come right
some day or night.
The moon is up, the sea is down,
and the world goes on spinning
round and round."

Jerry's song ended,
and he patted my back.
"Good night, Jack," said Jerry.
"Sweet dreams."

I gazed at the shining moon
until my eyelids grew heavy,
and then I fell asleep.
If only I had not slept!
Perhaps none of the rest of it
would have happened.

Chapter Two

Stolen!

I woke sharply.

The moon shone like a new coin.

What had awakened me?

A cloud passed over.

The night went dark.

Suddenly, rough hands grabbed me
and forced a cold steel bit
between my teeth.
A bridle went over my head
and pinched my ears.

Then a shadowy figure pulled me
from my stall and into the night.
I gave a frightened neigh,
but Jerry did not come.

"That's right, say good-bye,"
said a gruff voice.
"Tomorrow you'll have a new master,
and I'll make a pretty penny."

The horse thief laughed
and pulled harder on the reins.
We walked briskly away along the road.

I was terrified.

Even in my terror, I took care

to see where we were going.

I noticed things along the way—

a crooked tree in the moonlight,

a painted house,

a post with three signs.

We walked for miles and miles.

At last, the thief put me in a stall
with some sleeping horses.
Bone tired and afraid,
I heard the gate lock shut behind me.

Chapter Three
A Cruel Master

I woke to grumbling.

"Lousy horse fair,"

said a skinny gray mare.

"We'll all be sold by nightfall,"

said a dappled bay.

"Or worse," said the mare.

"We might be stuck with Blane

as our master.

He is a cruel man."

Just then, a gruff voice called out.
“This one will do.”
“It’s Blane!” said the mare
in a low nicker.
Now I saw that Blane was
the horse thief from last night.

He threw a rope around my neck
and led me out of the stall.

He put me to work
pulling a loaded cart.
The load was heavy.
My neck and shoulders hurt.
"Quickly, now," he said.

"You must be back in the stall
and looking rested when I sell you."
He snapped the whip by my ear,
one time, and then again.
Snap! Snap!

“Or maybe I’ll keep you,” Blane said.

I remembered

what the mare had told me,

and I tossed my mane in fear.

I did not want to be sold and

I did not want the cruel horse thief

to be my master.

Jerry! My heart cried out.

Jerry was my master!

I finished pulling the cart,
and Blane put me in the stall
without wiping my sweating flanks.

“Are you all right?” asked the dappled bay.

“Yes,” I whinnied, and thanked him.

But my mind was racing.

I had to get free!

Chapter Four

Escape!

Later, a boy opened the gate
and came in to feed us.
That is when I saw my chance.
The boy had been careless.
The gate was not quite shut.
The instant the boy's back was turned,
I charged out of the gate,
down the road, and away.

My heart beat Jerry, Jerry, Jerry!
in time with the pounding of my hooves.
Over the noise of my ragged breath
and racing hooves,
I heard horses galloping behind me
and men shouting.

I'd be caught

if I stayed on the road.

I bolted from the road and
crashed into the woods.
Branches scratched at my eyes,
and thorns scraped my legs.
I ran for a long time.
Finally, I had to stop.

My breathing slowed,

and I stood still to listen.

The woods were silent.

No one had followed me.

I had escaped!

But now I was hopelessly lost.

I tried to find a road.

I was hungry and thirsty.

I'd run too hard and too far,

and now my flanks twitched

and shivered with cold.

I walked for miles.

At last, I recognized a large rock,

and my hopes soared.

But a moment later,

I knew I'd seen the rock before.

I'd walked in circles.

I was no closer to home than

if I hadn't walked these long hours at all.

Night came, and so did the rain.
Cold and wet, I stumbled
under a rocky ledge.
Finally the rain stopped and
moonlight fell across a puddle
outside my rough shelter.

I thought of Jerry's song
about the moon and the sea
and the spinning world,
and in my mind, I heard his voice.
'Twill all come right
some day or night.
I took some small comfort,
and I fell asleep.

Chapter Five

Home Again

In the gray light of morning,

I went on my way again.

I was lost, cold, and tired.

I hardly knew which way to go.

Then something caught my eye.

Between the trees,

I saw a horse and cart drive by.

A road!

I followed the road a long way

but kept to the woods beside it.

A horse alone is in danger.

The sun was high
when at last I saw
a post with three signs.
I'd seen that post before.
I began to trot faster.

Soon I saw the painted house.

I picked up my pace.

There was the crooked tree!

I was getting close!

Then I heard something
that made my heart leap.
It was Jerry's voice.
He was singing.
Although I was tired,
I broke into a gallop.
I had never heard a sweeter sound.
I whinnied with joy,
and Jerry turned around.
"Jack!"

Jerry threw his arms around my neck.
"I've been looking for you
day and night!

"When I saw your bridle was gone,
I knew you'd been stolen."
I tossed my mane to tell him
he was right.
Jerry shook his head.
"I wonder how you found your way
home to me, Jack," he said.
"You must have kept
your wits about you."

I couldn't tell Jerry how his song
had comforted me,
so I rubbed his arm with my nose
and gave a gentle whinny.
Jerry smiled and hummed,
and together, we walked home
while Jerry sang the song I loved.

"Do your best and leave the rest,
'twill all come right
some day or night.
The moon is up, the sea is down,
and the world goes on spinning
round and round."